Gran and Bret's Trip!

Level 1E

Written by Isabel Crawford
Illustrated by Sue King

What is synthetic phonics?

Synthetic phonics teaches children to recognise the sounds of letters and to blend (synthesise) them together to make whole words.

Understanding sound/letter relationships gives children the confidence and ability to read unfamiliar words, without having to rely on memory or guesswork; this helps them progress towards independent reading.

Did you know? Spoken English uses more than 40 speech sounds. Each sound is called a *phoneme*. Some phonemes relate to a single letter (d-o-g) and others to combinations of letters (sh-ar-p). When a phoneme is written down it is called a *grapheme*. Teaching these sounds, matching them to their written form and sounding out words for reading is the basis of synthetic phonics.

Consultant

I love reading phonics has been created in consultation with language expert Abigail Steel. She has a background in teaching and teacher training and is a respected expert in the field of Synthetic Phonics. Abigail Steel is a regular contributor to educational publications. Her international education consultancy supports parents and teachers in the promotion of literacy skills.

Reading tips

This book focuses on:
ccvc words
(consonant-consonant-vowel-consonant)

Tricky words in this book

Any words in bold may have unusual spellings or are
new and have not yet been introduced.

> Tricky words in this book:
>
> ## go   the   what

Extra ways to have fun with with this book

• After the reader has read the story, ask them questions
about what they have just read:

What did Gran and Bret do on their trip?
How did Gran and Bret catch all the crabs in the end?

• Make flashcards of the ccvc words in this book. Ask
the reader to say the words, sounding them out. This
will help reinforce letter/sound matches.

> If Gran and Bret
> want to catch me, they'll
> have to get snappy!

A pronunciation guide

This grid contains the sounds used in
the story and a guide on how to say them.

s as in sat	a as in ant	t as in tin	p as in pig
i as in ink	n as in net	c as in cat	e as in egg
h as hen	r as in rat	m as in mug	d as in dog
g as in get	o as in ox	u as in up	l as in log
f as in fan	b as in bag	j as in jug	v as in van
w as in wet	z as in zip	y as in yet	k as in kit
qu as in quick	x as in box	ff as in off	ll as in ball
ss as in kiss	zz as in buzz	ck as in duck	

Be careful not to add an 'uh' sound to 's', 't', 'p',
'c', 'h', 'r', 'm', 'd', 'g', 'l', 'f' and 'b'. For example,
say 'fff' not 'fuh' and 'sss' not 'suh'.

Bret and Gran **go** on a trip.

Bret and Gran stop.

Gran has a kip.

Bret has a jog

and a swim.

Bret and Gran spot a crab.

They trap it in a box.

But **the** crab runs from the box!
Drat!

Quick! Can Bret grab the crab?

Will Gran grab the crab?

Bret and Gran can not
grab the crab!

The crab zips back in. Plop!

Bret is glum. **What** a loss.

Do not fret! Gran has a net.

Bret and Gran get lots of crabs!

What a trip!

OVER **48** TITLES IN SIX LEVELS
Abigail Steel recommends...

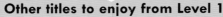

Other titles to enjoy from Level 1

I love reading phonics
Bad Rat

978-1-84898-277-2

I love reading phonics
The Best Gift

978-1-84898-396-0

I love reading phonics
Clint and Grant Play I-Spy

978-1-84898-548-3

Some titles from Level 2

I love reading phonics
Wish Fish

978-1-84898-386-1

I love reading phonics
Chuck and Duck

978-1-84898-387-8

I love reading phonics
Pink Bunny

978-1-84898-550-6

I love reading phonics
Let's go to the Swings

978-1-84898-549-0

Some titles from Level 3

I love reading phonics
Bart's Go-Cart

978-1-84898-552-0

I love reading phonics
Queen Ella's Feet

978-1-84898-398-4

I love reading phonics
Puff Flies

978-1-84898-399-1

I love reading phonics
The Pop Duet

978-1-84898-551-3

An Hachette UK Company
www.hachette.co.uk

Copyright © Octopus Publishing Group Ltd 2012
First published in Great Britain in 2012 by TickTock, a division of Octopus Publishing Group Ltd,
Endeavour House, 189 Shaftesbury Avenue, London WC2H 8JY.
www.octopusbooks.co.uk

ISBN 978 1 84898 547 6

Printed and bound in China
10 9 8 7 6 5 4 3 2 1